Dreaming of America

An Ellis Island Story

by Eve Bunting   illustrated by Ben F. Stahl

Troll

BridgeWater Books

For Ed, who brought me to the New World—E. B.

To my very supportive wife, Pat—B. F. S.

Deepwater Quay, Queenstown (now Cobh), County Cork, Ireland.
Annie Moore began her journey to America from this dock.

We gratefully acknowledge the following for their generous support and cooperation with us on this project: Cobh Heritage Centre, Cobh, County Cork, Ireland; The National Park Service, Statue of Liberty National Monument. Special thanks to Barry Moreno and Jeffrey Dosik at the Statue of Liberty/Ellis Island Research Library; The National Archives Varick Street Depository; and the National Library of Ireland.

Photo credits: page 2, courtesy of the National Library of Ireland, Lawrence Collection; page 7, courtesy of The Mariners' Museum; page 10, The National Archives; pages 17, 20, Corbis-Bettmann; pages 25, 29, 32 (left), by courtesy of the Ellis Island Immigration Museum; page 26, Mystic Seaport Museum, Inc.; page 32 (right), © Peter Zoeller.

Published by BridgeWater Books, an imprint and registered trademark of Troll Communications L.L.C.

Designed by Dorit Radandt and Shi Chen.   Printed in the United States of America.

10 9 8 7 6 5 4 3 2

Library of Congress Cataloging-in-Publication Data

Bunting, Eve.
Dreaming of America: an Ellis Island story / by Eve Bunting ; illustrations by Ben F. Stahl.
p.   cm.
Summary: Annie Moore cares for her two younger brothers on board the ship
sailing from Ireland to America, where she becomes the first immigrant processed
through Ellis Island, January 1, 1892, her fifteenth birthday.
ISBN 0-8167-6520-0
1. Moore, Annie, b. 1877–Juvenile fiction. [1. Moore, Annie, b. 1877–
Fiction. 2. Ocean travel–Fiction. 3. Emigration and immigration–
Fiction. 4. Irish Americans–Fiction. 5. Brothers and sisters–Fiction.]
I. Stahl, Ben F., ill. II. Title.
PZ7.B91527 Ds 1999
[E]–dc21   99-025708

The SS *Nevada* steamed out of the harbor and into the open seas. Her decks were abustle with men, women, and children, some still dragging their trunks and boxes.

Annie Moore and her brothers, Anthony and little Phillip, stood at the railing, watching Ireland disappear into the mist.

Gone, Annie thought. The word had the awfulest, loneliest sound.

Just last night she'd been dancing at the wake her friends had given for the leaving. There'd been sad farewells. But there'd been music and singing and laughter, too. And now her friends were lost to her forever.

"Will we be back, Annie?" Phillip asked.

Annie tightened her arms around her two little brothers. "I hope so."

Bad thoughts crowded into her mind. What if their mother and father weren't there to meet them when they landed in America? It was three years now since they'd seen their parents. For three years Annie and Phillip and Anthony had lived with Auntie and Uncle in the wee warm house in Cork that was truly home. Would she ever see it again? Would she ever see them again? She'd never forget the heartbreak in their faces as they'd said their last good-byes that very morning. Annie swallowed the tears that came with the memories.

"Annie?" Phillip touched her hand and turned his face up to hers. "I know what we can do, Annie. We can make a lot of money in America and send tickets for Auntie and Uncle the way Mammie and Daddy sent them for us."

A man leaning on the rail next to Phillip asked, "Are you traveling alone?"

"No. I've got our Annie and Anthony," Phillip said.

The man smiled. "I meant, without parents."

"They're waiting for us in America," Annie told him. She liked the look of him. He was older than her uncle, small as a bird in his brown tweed jacket. He wore a soft hat that drooped back and front, and he had a red bow tie that perched on the point of his Adam's apple. He took off his hat. "I am Viktor Kirschenblatt, from Russia. I boarded ship at Liverpool."

Annie bobbed her head. "We're pleased to meet you, Mr. Kirschen . . ."

"Call me Mr. Viktor, please. Will be easier."

They shook hands. The boys, too.

The *Nevada* gave a lurch as a swell hit it, and Anthony held on to Annie's arm. "There's no land behind us anymore," he said in a scared voice.

"And none in front," Mr. Viktor said. "Just water and promise of America."

They faced the ship's bow as it plowed and bored into the gray ocean. Annie shivered. Her new suit was not warm, and the boots Auntie had bought for her were thin, too. She pulled her short jacket close about her. "May we ask why you are going to America, Mr. Viktor?"

"I have son in Philadelphia." He shrugged. "It is also very dangerous to be Jew in Russia."

"Can you teach us Russian?" Anthony asked.

"Da." He smiled. "That means 'yes.' Perhaps a few words. You would like?"

"Da," Anthony said.

Annie hugged her arms about herself. "'Tis ever so cold. I should take my brothers below."

"We will meet again," Mr. Viktor said.

The SS Nevada *brought immigrants from Europe to America from 1869 to 1894. In 1896 the* Nevada *was taken out of commission and scrapped in Italy.*

Annie held tight to her brothers' hands as they leaned against the wind that whistled along the deck. She pushed open a door to the stairs, and they made their way down, down, down, past several decks lined with cabin doors.

Anthony clutched at Annie's arm.

"Are we below the ocean, Annie?"

"We are. Isn't it exciting?"

"Can the water not get in?"

"Not at all. No more than the rain could get in our house at home." She was checking the numbers on each cabin against the label they'd been given as they boarded. "Here we are. You open the door, Phillip."

They stood, staring into the cabin.

"Isn't this the nice wee room, now?" Annie asked shakily. "Cozy. Just for the three of us."

In truth, it wasn't cozy, and not that nice, either. There were no windows in their cabin. The only furniture was a washstand with a mirror over it and three iron beds, two of them stacked one on top of the other. Annie longed for the poppy wallpaper in their little attic bedroom at home. She longed, too, for the smell of the mothballs Auntie kept in their wardrobe. She'd never thought she'd miss the smell of mothballs.

"Can I have the bed on top?" Phillip asked, beginning to monkey climb.

Annie pulled him back. "You may not. I don't want you falling on your head. I'll be up there, and you'll be below me. Anthony will have the bed against the wall."

"What's that noise?" Little Phillip held his hands over his ears.

"It's the big engines that make the ship go," Annie shouted. "I think we're right on top of them."

In the corridor outside, babies cried, trunks scratched along the floor. A voice called, "Bridget?" And someone answered, "Save us all. We'll be suffocated down here. 'Tis like being in a coffin." A cabin door slammed.

Their bag with the third-class label was sitting by the door. Beside it was the brown paper parcel Auntie had handed to them before they left. "For Christmas," she'd whispered. "A wee bit of home. And a little something inside for your birthday, too, Acushla. You can open it on the big ship the day you become fifteen." She'd hugged Annie tight. "And think of us, darlin'."

"I'll think of you always," Annie had said, speaking through the thickness of her throat. "Always."

She opened the suitcase now and removed the two pictures she'd taken off the wall of their bedroom. There'd been white patches on the poppy wallpaper where they'd hung for so long. One was of their mother and father. The other was of Auntie and Uncle. She set them on the washstand.

"There," she said. "Now we'll not be so lonesome."

Phillip started to cry. "I want to go home," he sobbed.

Annie rocked him against her. "It'll be all right, so," she murmured. "Aren't we going to our new home in America?"

SS Nevada *passenger list. Annie and her brothers are passengers two through four. Note that Annie's "calling," or occupation, is listed as spinster, which means she was an unmarried woman.*

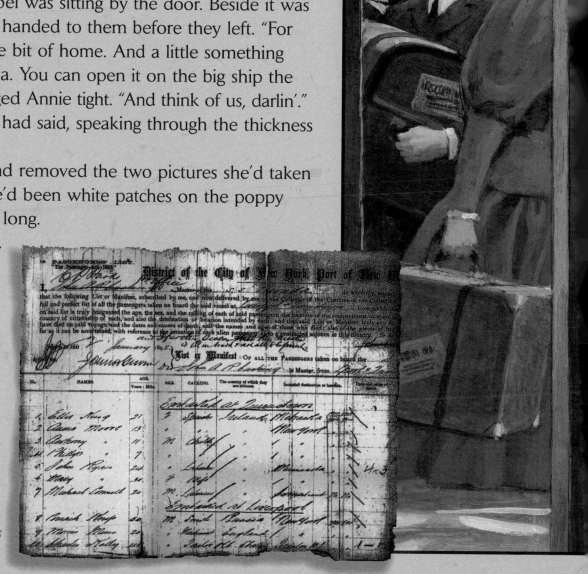

Mr. Viktor was their special companion during the voyage.

"I take you under my feathers," he told Anthony, and Anthony giggled.

"You mean 'wing,'" he said.

Mr. Viktor groaned. "I try hard not to make mistake."

"You speak grand," Annie said. "What is Russian for 'friend'?"

"The word in English is good." Mr. Viktor smiled. "I like that you use it."

He sat next to them at the big wooden table where they ate their food. There were plenty of potatoes and bread. One night there was stew.

"Not like Auntie makes." Anthony spat a knot of gristle into his hand.

After the third day, it didn't matter what food they got. None of them were eating.

A great storm had blown up, and the ship rolled and lurched. The seas battered and smashed across its decks. Nobody could go outside, and the smell of sick was everywhere. The ocean heaved, the ship heaved, and every stomach aboard heaved with it.

In the cabin, there was no escape from the banging of the engines. It pounded in their ears day and night. They were so close to the bow, they could feel every thump and slurp of the ship meeting the waves.

"Are we going to die, Annie?" Little Phillip's face was the pale green of the underside of a leaf.

"No, Acushla. We're safe as can be." She wiped sweat from his forehead. What if little Phillip died here, in the middle of this awful ocean?

"It'll pass, lovey. It will," Anthony groaned.

Night and day she watched over them, dragging herself down from her top bed to hold them and to pray.

Mr. Viktor brought drinking water to their cabin. Once, he brought a bowl of soup, big enough for the three of them.

"Where did you get it?" Annie asked.

"I have made a friend of steward in first class," Mr. Viktor said. "He is also Russian. He tells me that even the rich are not eating in this storm."

We are under his feathers, Annie thought, and we are safer when they are covering us.

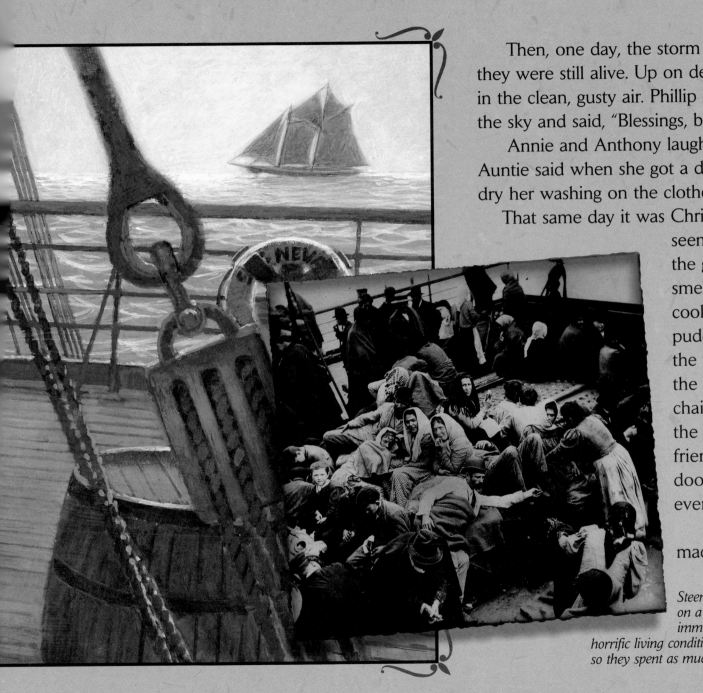

Then, one day, the storm was over. And they were still alive. Up on deck, they breathed in the clean, gusty air. Phillip lifted his face to the sky and said, "Blessings, blessings, blessings."

Annie and Anthony laughed. That was what Auntie said when she got a day without rain to dry her washing on the clothesline.

That same day it was Christmas. But it didn't seem real. Where was the good Christmas smell of the goose cooking? And the plum pudding simmering on the fire? Where were the colored paper chains hanging from the ceiling and the friends coming to the door? How could this ever be Christmas?

But it was, and they made the best of it.

Steerage passengers huddled on a ship's deck. Many poor immigrants had to endure horrific living conditions in the bowels of ships, so they spent as much time as possible on deck.

Down in their cabin, the boys sat on Anthony's bed, one on each side of Annie, and she untied the string on Auntie's parcel. On top was a letter.

"My dear children," it began:

> My dear children,
>
> By now your uncle and I will know how much we miss you. You are like our own and you always will be. God keep you safe.
>
> Happy Christmas.

There was a scarf for each of them, a red one for Anthony, yellow for Phillip, and blue for Annie.

"When did she ever knit these?" Annie asked. "I didn't see her making them."

Phillip pulled aside the rest of the paper. "There's more!" Wrapped in a cloth were three mince pies, plump with currants and raisins.

"I want my auntie!" Phillip wailed, rubbing his eyes.

"Now, now. Isn't it the grand thing that we're well enough to eat what she sent? Take a bite, Phillip, and enjoy your Christmas."

"Aren't you going to have yours, Annie?"

"I'm keeping it for Mr. Viktor," Annie said. "I have nothing else for him."

Anthony held out his pie. "Here. Have a bite of mine."

"And take a bite of mine," Phillip added. "But only a wee bite, Annie."

"You are dear boys." Annie held each taste in her mouth for as long as she could before swallowing.

Never was a mince pie so good!
She picked up a juicy currant that
had fallen on the blanket and
popped it in her mouth.

The last little twist of paper
was so small they almost missed
it. "For Annie," it said. "Happy
fifteenth birthday."

Little Phillip bounced on the
bed, making it rattle. "Open it,
Annie. Open it."

Annie slid the package under
her pillow. "I won't be fifteen for
seven more days. Auntie said I
should save it 'til then. Let's go
now and find Mr. Viktor. Put on
your coats and scarves. Aren't
they lovely and warm? I'm not
sure if Jewish gentlemen keep
Christmas. We can just tell him
we wanted to share what we got
from home."

Anthony nodded. "We can
wish him a happy Halfway-to-
America Day. From all of us."

After Christmas, the weather was fine. Sun glittered on the ocean, and at night the moon spilled a shining path that shimmered to the horizon.

"We could walk on it all the way back home," Anthony said.

Annie felt a sharp pang at her heart, but all she said was, "Then our mother and father would be terrible sad."

One night, there was a party in steerage, with an accordion playing music from home and from other countries far from Ireland. There were reels and polkas and jigs. Mr. Viktor danced with Annie in a stiff old-gentleman way that she loved.

It was the day after that a seagull flew over the SS *Nevada* and landed on one of the masts. "That means we come close to land," Mr. Viktor told them.

Annie shivered. Close to America and all its strangeness.

On the last night of 1891, the night before Annie's fifteenth birthday, the engines stopped and there was silence. In the windowless cabin, there was no way to see what was happening.
But when they rushed into the corridor, a steward turned them
back. "No steerage passengers allowed on deck,"
he said.

"Are we there?" Annie asked.

"We are. But nobody gets off 'til morning. And none of you from steerage are allowed up 'til then."

After the never-ending noise, the quiet in the cabin was almost unbearable. Anthony and Phillip slept while Annie lay awake. Were their parents looking out at their ship? How would it be when they met after all this time? What would New York be like? Number 32 Monroe Street? She'd tried for so long to imagine it.

Immigrants brought music from their homelands to America. Music kept them connected to those that were left behind.

They knew it was morning when the steward banged on their door and shouted, "Get your things together. Everybody up on deck."

"Dress yourselves *extra* warm now," Annie told her little brothers. "Put on your woolen vests. It's colder here than in Cork."

Excitement fumbled their fingers, and Annie had to help them with their buttons.

Phillip flung himself at her. "Annie? Did you forget it's your birthday? Open your present before we go."

"I will. But hush up. I have to get it." Annie took the curl of paper from the pocket of her suit, where she'd put it the night before. She sat on Anthony's bed to open it.

Anthony's eyes widened. "It's Auntie's lovely ring."

Annie stared down at it. The two little red hearts joined together gleamed even in the gloom of the cabin. So often she'd seen the ring on Auntie's hand. "They're not rubies," her auntie had said one time. "But your uncle gave me this ring when we were courting, and it's precious above rubies to me."

Now it was Annie's. Her heart was full to bursting as she slid it on her finger. It was a perfect fit.

There was another bang on the door. "Do you want to be left behind?"

Not one of them looked back as they hurried from the dark mouse hole of a cabin. Up the stairs, up and up, bumping their bag behind them.

The outside morning was filled with wind and sunshine. The decks were crowded. Annie saw two other ships at anchor in the harbor. In the distance were buildings, and a wharf where small boats were moored, and people who looked no bigger than blades of grass.

"Is that America?" little Phillip asked.

"'Tis."

And there was the statue. Annie dropped her bag and put her arms tight around her brothers. "There she is," she whispered. "The Statue of Liberty. Our daddy wrote about her. Remember? Isn't she grand altogether?"

Some of the passengers were on their knees. One man kept pointing and calling out, "Bella! Bella!"

Mr. Viktor had come to stand beside them. "'Bella' means 'beautiful' in Italian," he said. "My son say she is truly called Liberty Enlightening the World. Is very nice, I think."

Annie nodded. "She is bella. Very, very bella."

Mr. Viktor pointed. "That land is Ellis Island. We will go to the building, the one flying the big flag."

The original Ellis Island immigration building was completed in 1891. It was destroyed by fire in 1897. The building that now stands on Ellis Island was completed in 1900.

As he spoke, one of the small moored boats began moving in their direction. It was strung, bow to stern, with red and blue bunting, and it seemed to bounce across the harbor. Water danced and feathered behind it.

Annie pressed her hands against her cheeks. "Oh, look what it's called. It's the *John E. Moore*."

Phillip gasped. "Is it our boat, Annie? Did Mammie and Daddy buy it for us coming?"

Annie laughed. "I don't think so, wee Phillip. There must be another man called Moore who is famous in America."

The *John E. Moore* tied up next to the SS *Nevada*, and at once the passengers began to board the little boat that would ferry them into port.

For a few minutes the smaller boat bobbed against the bigger ship, as if waiting for a signal. And then, on the distant wharf, a giant flag was lowered and raised three times. The *John E. Moore* sounded a happy toot and set off for shore.

Annie held tight to her brothers' hands.

The cheers from the wharf got louder the closer they got. Do they always greet newcomers like this? Annie wondered. It was remarkable.

"Do you see them yet?" Anthony stood on tiptoe. His hand in Annie's was cold as pond ice.

"What will we do if Mammie and Daddy aren't here?" Little Phillip buried his face in Annie's skirt.

What if we don't recognize each other? Annie worried. But she didn't say.

"They will be there," she told Phillip. "And if not, you have me. Do you think I can't find thirty-two Monroe Street, me that has got you so far? Me that's fifteen?"

The boat nosed into the dock, and its engines stopped. Whistles whistled. Bells rang. Voices screamed out names: "Hans! Jasmine! Françoise!"

The *John E. Moore* was one of the steamboats that ferried third-class passengers to Ellis Island for processing. First- and second-class passengers were quickly processed on board ship.

Annie faced Mr. Viktor. "When we go from here, will we see you again?"

"Philadelphia is not far from New York. We can arrange." He lifted Annie's hand to his lips. "One does not ever lose friend."

With a squeak and a squeal, the gangplank was lowered.

Mr. Viktor gave Annie a little push. "Be first, Annie. First will be good."

A man in an overcoat with a shawl wrapped in folds around his neck moved in front of them. Close to Annie, another man yanked at the shawl, pulling him back. "Ladies first," he said in an Irish brogue. "You step out, little lady."

Annie stepped out, Anthony and Phillip at her heels.

The cheers were like thunder. Small American flags waved. Hats and caps flew in the air. The salty air smelled good. The smell of America.

Two important-looking gentlemen in suits took her hands. "Welcome. You are the first immigrant to enter our country through Ellis Island," one of the gentlemen said.

"First will be good," Mr. Viktor had said. This was what he'd meant. This was why there was a big celebration!

"I am Colonel Weber," the other gentleman said. "What is your name?"

Annie tried not to stammer. "I am Annie Moore of Cork, Ireland. These are my brothers, Anthony and Phillip." She stood, unsure and embarrassed, knowing everyone was watching them. All those hundreds of people pressed behind the barricades. She looked from side to side. Oh, if she could only see her parents!

"We want you to accept this ten-dollar gold piece to commemorate this important day in history," Colonel Weber said.

"And it's Annie's birthday, too," little Phillip piped up.

An important day in history, and she was a part of it! Annie stared down at the gold coin. It seemed to float in her hand, bright as sunshine. Ten dollars? That must be a fortune!

"I'll never part with it. Never," she whispered.

"Now, if you and your brothers will come with us, we will get you registered. . . ."

Colonel John Weber, Superintendent of Immigration

It was then Annie heard the shouts, so excited they rose above the noise around them.

"It's little Annie and little Anthony and little Phillip!"

"Daddy!" Annie called. "Daddy!" She'd know that voice anywhere. That was the voice that was strict when he helped her with her sums, soft when he called her his own wee love. How could she have thought she'd ever forget it?

And there was her mother, pushing through to the front of the crowd, her face red with excitement, her hat and hair every which way. "Here we are, darlin's, here we are!" she called.

"I see them!" Anthony stretched his arms toward them and then hefted Phillip up so he could see, too.

"I remember them exactly," he whispered to Annie. "I remember Mammie's green coat with the bone buttons. I didn't know I remembered."

They waved and waved.

"How does it feel to be in America?" a man with a notepad asked.

"Grand altogether," Annie said. She looked down at her ring with the red stones that were more precious than rubies. The two hearts. Ireland and America. Was that what her auntie had known when she gave it?

I am Annie Moore of Cork, Ireland, she thought. And I am Annie Moore of America.

Afterword

Annie Moore was the first immigrant to be processed through Ellis Island, on January 1, 1892, her fifteenth birthday. She and her two brothers had made the journey to America to be reunited with their parents, Matt and Mary Moore, in New York City. Several years later the Moore family settled in Indiana.

When she was twenty-one, Annie moved to Texas and married Patrick O'Connell. They had five children. This much of Annie's story is true.

Little else is known of the young Irish girl with her "pink cheeks and auburn hair" who now symbolizes the many millions of Irish who left their homeland for new lives in America.

A statue of Annie and her brothers stands on the quay at Cobh (pronounced COVE), Ireland, where their journey began. Another stands on Ellis Island, where their journey ended.

This is a fictionalized telling of how the voyage might have been for Annie, imagined with much affection by the author, who herself left Ireland for America in 1958.

This is the real Annie Moore with her firstborn child, Mary Catherine.

The Annie Moore statue at Cobh, Ireland, is a poignant reminder of the millions of Irish people who left their homeland, families, and friends.